Wandering Wind

Copyright © 2013 M. H. Kirmani & B. P. Laster

Library of Congress Control Number:
ISBN-13 978-1482587005
ISBN-10 1482587009

No part of this publication may be reproduced, stored in a retrieval system, or transmitted in any form or by any means, electronic, mechanical, photocopying, recording, or otherwise, without written permission of the author/publisher. For information regarding permission, write to mkirmani@towson.edu or blaster@towson.edu.

Second Edition, July 2013.

We dedicate this book to
Laura, Nabeel, Abigail, Muneer, Talia, and Kabir.

We are deeply grateful for the technical support of Sheri Muncy.

We extend our appreciation to
the Interfaith Conference of Metropolitan Washington
for their feedback and support.

The sun was shining and big
white clouds dotted the sky
on one cool, breezy day
in fall.

4

Daniel, Yasmin, Nicole, and Joginder
were on the playground,
leaping off and on the spinning
whirl-around and jumping into piles
of crackly, golden leaves.

5

The children felt a big
gust of wind on their faces.
"Oh no,
my kippah has flown off!"
exclaimed Daniel.
Everyone chased
the round
cloth cap that
Daniel
usually
wore on his head.

6

"Here you go, Daniel," said Joginder,
as he handed him the kippah.
Yasmin offered, "Here, Daniel. I have an extra
hairclip. You can use it to hold your kippah
on your head."
"Thanks!" replied Daniel, as he secured the
head covering.

"Joginder, you don't have to worry about your head covering
blowing off!" Daniel remarked.
"Yeah," replied Joginder. "I wear a patka now, and when I get
older I will wear a full turban like my Dad."

7

Nicole looked at her three friends:
Daniel with a kippah,
Joginder with a patka,
and Yasmin with a hijab and she asked,
"Why do you always wear something
on your head?"

"It reminds us to follow the ways of our families,"
explained Joginder.
Daniel and Yasmin nodded in agreement.

"I don't wear anything on my head,
so I guess that is my family's way.
My aunt, though, wears a
beautiful lace mantilla, like a headscarf,
when she goes to church on Sundays.
Then, she is just like the rest of you!"
exclaimed Nicole.

9

As the wind kept blowing, Yasmin retrieved something colorful from her backpack. The friends smiled as Yasmin handed each one of them a shiny pinwheel. Soon, all four pin-wheels were spinning swiftly in the wind.

Suddenly, tumbling down in the blowing wind came a purple beetle.

Nicole noticed it first and ran to look at it.
"Look, a beetle wiggling its legs!"
The rest of the children followed and surrounded the insect.
The beetle had landed on its back.

The beetle tried to turn over, but all it could do was to kick its legs in the air. Daniel asked, "How can we help it to turn over? Maybe we can pick it up?"

"Be careful, it might sting," warned Joginder.

Nicole reminded the others, "Yes, don't touch it with your hands."

Yasmin added, "Also, we don't want to hurt it. The wind must have blown it down from the tree."

The children wondered how best to help the beetle.
It lay helplessly on the ground, furiously wiggling its legs.

Joginder piped up, "Let's use something to turn it over. Here, I found a long piece of straw."
"Okay, let's work together to do it." Nicole suggested.

As they brought the straw closer to the beetle, it tried to clasp the straw with its legs. The straw went limp. The beetle slipped and fell. Yasmin gasped, "Oh no, it has fallen back again!"

14

"Maybe there will be another gust of wind
that will help the beetle to turn over,"
said Daniel. As the children waited
for the wind to pick up again,
they watched the beetle and
thought about what the wind can do.
Nicole spoke, "The
wind can scatter
seeds everywhere.
Look at the
dandelions
blowing."

The wind kept blowing and the children started
"Whooo. . . ing" into it, louder and then softer.
"The wind helps us in so many ways.
It carries the sounds of our voices so that we can
hear and listen to each other!" bellowed Nicole.

Yasmin brought the group's attention back to the beetle. "I wish the wind would blow stronger so that the beetle could turn over onto its legs."

Joginder remarked, "What about if we create some artificial wind?"
"How?" chorused Nicole, Yasmin and Daniel.
"Does anyone have a fan?" asked Yasmin.
"No, but we can make one from folded paper. Look, I'll show you how," said Nicole excitedly.

Four sheets of notebook paper were taken out of four backpacks. Nicole showed the others how to fold the paper back and forth to make a fan.

Joginder said,
"Okay. Let's all flap
the fans at the same time."
The children squatted on all sides
of the beetle and waved the fans. A
breeze arose from the flapping
papers, but it seemed to
have no effect on the
unhappy beetle.

"We need to make stronger wind,
so it will help the beetle turn over,"
explained Daniel.
"Okay, I have a big wind in my breath!"
offered Nicole, as she blew on the beetle.
"Blow harder!" suggested Joginder.
Yasmin also tried to do the
same thing from where
she was sitting. The beetle
slid a little, but did not
turn over.

"How about if we all blow on it
.. but this time all of us from the same direction?"
cried out Yasmin. They all lined up at the head of
the beetle. Nicole shouted, "Okay, one, two, three . . ."
Each of the children took a very deep breath.
At the count of three, they all blew together on the beetle
from the same direction.

The children's efforts at creating wind
power, plus the beetle's squirming,
worked! The beetle turned over on its
legs, fluttered its wings,
and flew off.

The children laughed and cheered. "Goodbye!" they yelled after the beetle, hoping that the wind would carry all of their voices up to the sky and beyond.

25

A Note to Parents and Teachers

The Series

This book is part of a series that focuses on contemporary children living in a diverse community. A prominent feature of the books is a focus on the commonalities among children. They play on the playground, they solve problems, and they are friends. Thus, the books highlight both similarities and differences among the children, within particular family traditions and across religions and cultures.

There is no intent to impose religious beliefs or practices. Rather, our purpose is to raise awareness about different traditions. All cultures and religious traditions are valued. In fact, it is our belief that we can practice different theologies and rituals, and still respect that others faithfully and joyfully follow a different path. One thing that is special about these books is that we come to see—through the eyes of the children—that there are some commonalities across all of the religions, even though they are distinct from each other. Our intention is to plant the seed that may flower into greater understanding among children.

We hope that by reading aloud these books, we will engage children with each other, with their families, and with their teachers to explore their own realities.

This Book

Across the books in the series, many different religions, cultures, and traditions are featured. In *Wandering Wind,* the children are Muslim, Sikh, Christian, and Jewish. Running through the narrative of *Wandering Wind* is the theme of how head coverings are common in many different religious or cultural traditions. Here are some prompts to get your conversations at home or in the classroom started...

1. How are the children in the book similar to each other?
2. What differences can we see among the children?
3. What are some different head coverings or special outfits that people who you know wear?
4. If you do know anyone who wears a head covering or a hat, why does he/she wear it?
5. Where in the story do the children show concern or care?
6. What problem do the children solve?
7. In what different ways did they work together to solve the problem?
8. Can you think of a project that you have done with others to solve a problem?
9. What are some properties of wind and for what do we use wind?
10. When you think of the wind, what images come to mind?
11. What would have happened to the beetle if the children had not helped?

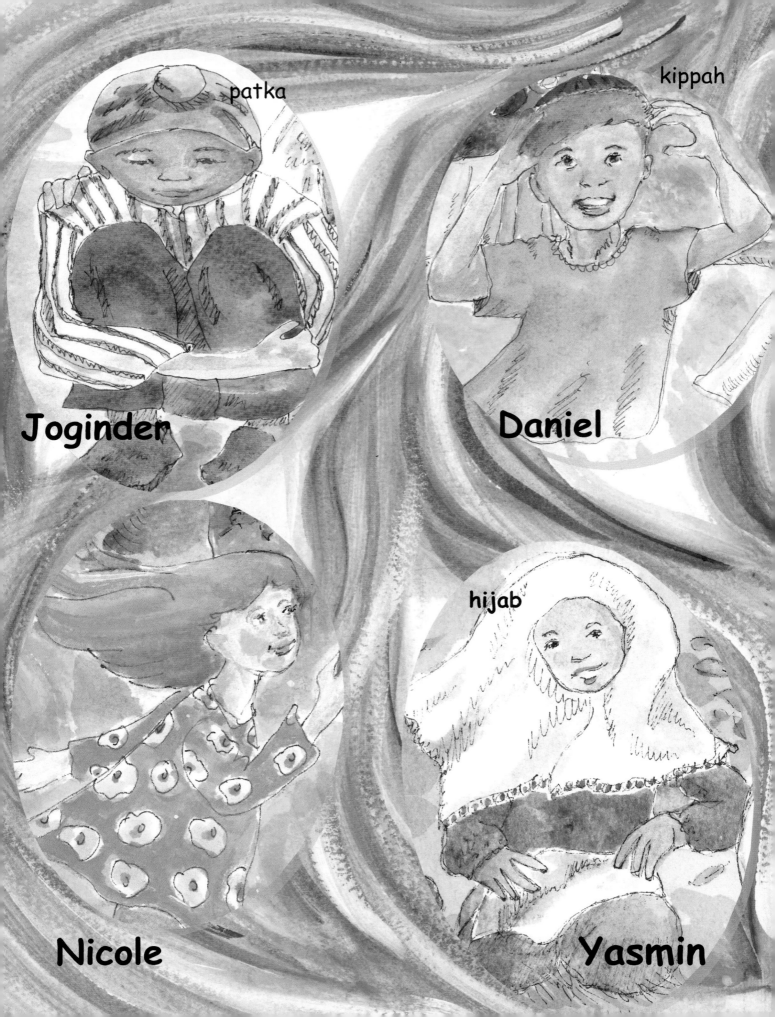

patka

kippah

Joginder

Daniel

Nicole

hijab

Yasmin

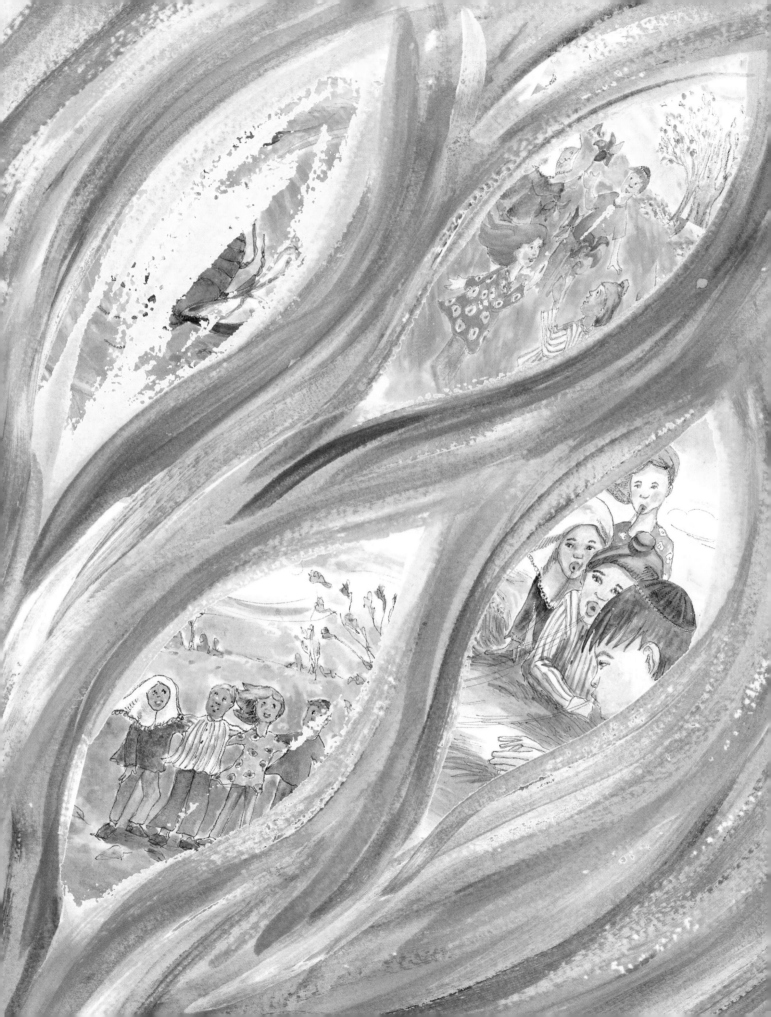

65318444R00018

Made in the USA
Charleston, SC
20 December 2016